MARCELLA'S HOUSE
W9-BXQ-145
PLAYHOUSE
TOOL SHED
PLAYROOM

This book belongs to:

Raggedy Ann & Andy's

WHAT CAN A CAMEL DO?

A LYNX BOOK

 ISBN: 1-55802-105-1 0 9 8 7 6 5 4 3 2

This book is published by Lynx Books, a division of Lynx Communications, Inc., 41 Madison Avenue, New York, New York 10010.

One morning the sparrows from the Deep Deep Woods fluttered about the playroom window. They had brought a special message all the way from Raggedy Land.

When the dolls heard the sparrows singing, they rushed to the window.

“Oh, look!” said Raggedy Ann, who was reading the invitation the sparrows had brought. “There’s going to be a special show in Raggedy Land tomorrow,” she announced. “It’s a talent show, and we’re all invited to perform.”

“What is a ‘talent show’?” asked Tim the Toy Soldier.

“It’s a show where everyone gets to do the thing he or she does best,” replied Raggedy Ann.

"And the thing we each do best is our special *talent!*" added Raggedy Andy.

"Oh, I see," Bubbles the Clown Doll said excitedly. "Magic tricks are my special talent—and that's what I would do in the talent show—if I were going to be in it, that is. . . ." he said uncertainly.

"Oh, let's be in the talent show," said Sunny Bunny. Marcella won't be home tomorrow, so we can go!" he said, hopping up and down.

"Oh yes," said the other dolls, and each began to plan a special thing to do.

All the dolls were very excited—all except The Camel with the Wrinkled Knees. He wasn't excited, because he didn't think he had a special talent. And if he didn't have a talent, he couldn't be in the show!

The Camel wondered if there was something special he could do. He decided to see what everyone else was planning, hoping that would give him a good idea.

Since the talent show was the very next day, the dolls were all practicing very hard.

"Toot, toot, toot-toot-toot. Toot, toot!" Percy the Policeman Doll played a tooting tune on his police whistle.

Bubbles the Clown Doll rubbed his white-gloved hands together, and PRESTO! He magically pulled a string of colorful handkerchiefs from his sleeve.

"Bubbles and Percy sure are good at what they do," The Camel with the Wrinkled Knees said to himself. "But tooting and magic just aren't for me," he sighed as he slowly walked away.

Just then Raggedy Andy tumbled by. Raggedy Andy loved to do somersaults. He could do ten in a row! And that's exactly what Raggedy Andy intended to do in the Raggedy Land talent show.

“My, that looks like fun,” The Camel called after Raggedy Andy. “Maybe I could do a tumble, too,” he thought hopefully. He waited until Raggedy Andy was a fair distance away and then he tried to tumble.

The Camel tried to bend over. But his head didn't quite touch the floor.

His body wouldn't roll. His legs folded at the knees. He discovered that tumbling just wasn't the thing for a camel whose knees were wrinkled.

So The Camel stood up and brushed himself off. He still didn't know what he was going to do for the show.

Then The Camel saw Babette the French Doll and Greta the Dutch Doll practicing their act. He walked over to watch them while they worked.

"Babette's song is nice," thought The Camel as he listened to her play her silver flute. But he knew that a camel could never play the flute like that.

"Clickety-clack, clickety-clack," tapped Greta's wooden clogs, as she danced a little Dutch dance to Babette's French song.

"Maybe I could do a little dance," The Camel thought hopefully. Then he backed into a corner and tried to clickety-clack the way that Greta did. But his front legs went in one direction and his back legs in another.

"I guess a camel's special talent isn't dancing a Dutch doll's dance," The Camel sighed in a disappointed way.

Then he sat himself down. He really needed to think.

While The Camel sat and thought, he listened to Raggedy Ann play "Twinkle, Twinkle, Little Star" on Marcella's toy piano. *Ping, ping. Ping, ping. Ping, ping, ping.* The notes rang out loud and clear. And Raggedy Dog and Raggedy Cat sang the words.

“Now that’s an idea,” The Camel said happily. “If Raggedy Dog and Raggedy Cat can sing, perhaps I can, too.”

The Camel had never sung before, and he didn't quite know how. By this time, he was willing to give anything a try. So he took a deep breath, and then he tried to sing with all his heart. But it didn't take very long for The Camel with the Wrinkled Knees to discover that he could not carry a tune!

Disappointed, The Camel just didn't know what to do next. Then from behind him came a very strange noise. *Boing. Boing. Boing.*

The Camel looked around. He looked up. He looked down. Then he noticed Sunny Bunny, hopping higher than ever before.

"My goodness, Sunny Bunny, you really can hop high," said The Camel admiringly.

"It's Marcella's . . . toy . . . trampoline . . .," explained Sunny Bunny breathlessly. "I'm practicing . . . my hopping . . .," he added. Then he disappeared from sight.

"So I see," said The Camel with a sigh.

Then The Camel with the Wrinkled Knees slowly walked away. He went and sat in a corner.

"There must be something a camel can do," he whispered softly to himself. And he tried to think of the things that he liked to do best.

A

"I like to take long walks," he thought to himself, remembering how much he enjoyed the long walks to Raggedy Land.

"And I like to give the other dolls rides on my back," he thought.

“But those are not the kinds of things a camel can do in a talent show. I’m afraid I’ll never think of something to do.”

That evening, after Marcella had gone to bed, the dolls whispered to each other about the talent show. They were so excited that they thought they would never be able to go to sleep.

But one by one, the exhausted dolls finally fell asleep. All except The Camel. He stayed awake all night, thinking and worrying about what he could do at the talent show.

The next day, the dolls in the playroom started packing up everything they needed for the show. Nobody noticed that The Camel didn't have anything to pack.

When everything was ready, the dolls stopped and stared at the big heap of stuff.

"Oh, dear," said Raggedy Ann, as she gazed at the pile in dismay. "How will we ever get all these things to Raggedy Land?"

Nobody knew what to do. Nobody except The Camel, that is.

“I know!” said The Camel. “If you strap all your things on my back, I can carry them to the talent show and bring them back home again.”

“What a wonderful idea!” said Raggedy Ann. And all the other dolls agreed.

"Hurray for The Camel with the Wrinkled Knees!" shouted Sunny Bunny.

So they packed up the piano, the balls, the flute, the trampoline, and all the other things they needed, and off they trooped to Raggedy Land.

And no one had a better time than The Camel with the Wrinkled Knees. In fact, the other dolls gave him a special prize for his special talent—being a helpful friend. Without The Camel, the playroom dolls would not have been able to take part in the talent show at all.

MOST
HELPFUL

RAGGEDY LAND
HOLE IN FENCE
DEEP DEEP WOODS